Publisher's Note: In keeping with one of the ideas in this story, that all things are just as they should be, the hand-drawn illustrations and text have been left with natural flaws to highlight the beauty of imperfection.

Irons in the Fire Press
First printing
Copyright © 2021 by Stacy Davies

ISBN: 978-0-578-33804-0

Printed in the United States of America.

This book is dedicated to

Nellie May McDonald Stewart

to whom we both owe so much

Early one morning when she rolled out of bed,
Maribelle Mansion rubbed her eyes and her head.
She looked at the sun through her window
and sighed thinking,
"Who am I today? Today, who am I?"

If the day were for school,
she'd have to become
a classmate,
a pupil,
a schoolyard chum.

If the day were for playing,
she'd have to become
a neighborhood friend
and explorer of fun!

To her mom and her dad,
she was daughter and child.
To her aunties and uncles,
a niece slightly wild!

To strangers she passed
on her outings to town,
she was a little green dress
that jumped up and down!

But none of these names
seemed to fit her at all.
She knew she was skinny,
she knew she was small.
When she looked in the mirror,
she saw her dark curls,
Her lashes and lips—
she felt like a girl.

But whenever she'd sit
very quiet and still,
just looking at pebbles,
or grass on a hill,
or watch as a ladybug
crawled cross her hand,
or make endless circles
with her finger in sand,

or notice the ripples
in a puddle or pond,
or hear the birds chirping
brightly at dawn,

or gaze at the stars
that sparkled each night,
or stare as the moon rose,

ghostly and bright,

or study the shapes
of the clouds in the sky,
she'd forget all her names,
and just think,
"Who am I?"

"Who am I inside?

Inside, who am I?

Am I more than just Maribelle?

Is Maribelle I?

Who is the me without names,

without words?

Am I like the butterflies?

Am I like the birds?"

"Am I like the wind
that roars through the trees?
Am I like animals,
the soil and the seeds?"

"Am I like the moon,
the stars and the sun?
Are we all the same?
In some way, are we one?"
And the more that she let
all the names float away,
and the thoughts of who
she must become on that day,

She knew that "Maribelle"

was only a name,

that kids and adults

were really the same.

That clothes and that hair

didn't matter at all,

or if you were little

or if you were tall.

She knew there was something
the eye couldn't see,
a thing deep inside
that was bigger than "me."
A thing that connects
all of heaven and earth,
A thing that is shared
from the moment of birth.

And she opened her eyes
with a smile and a sigh, and thought,
"I am all things —
and all things am I."

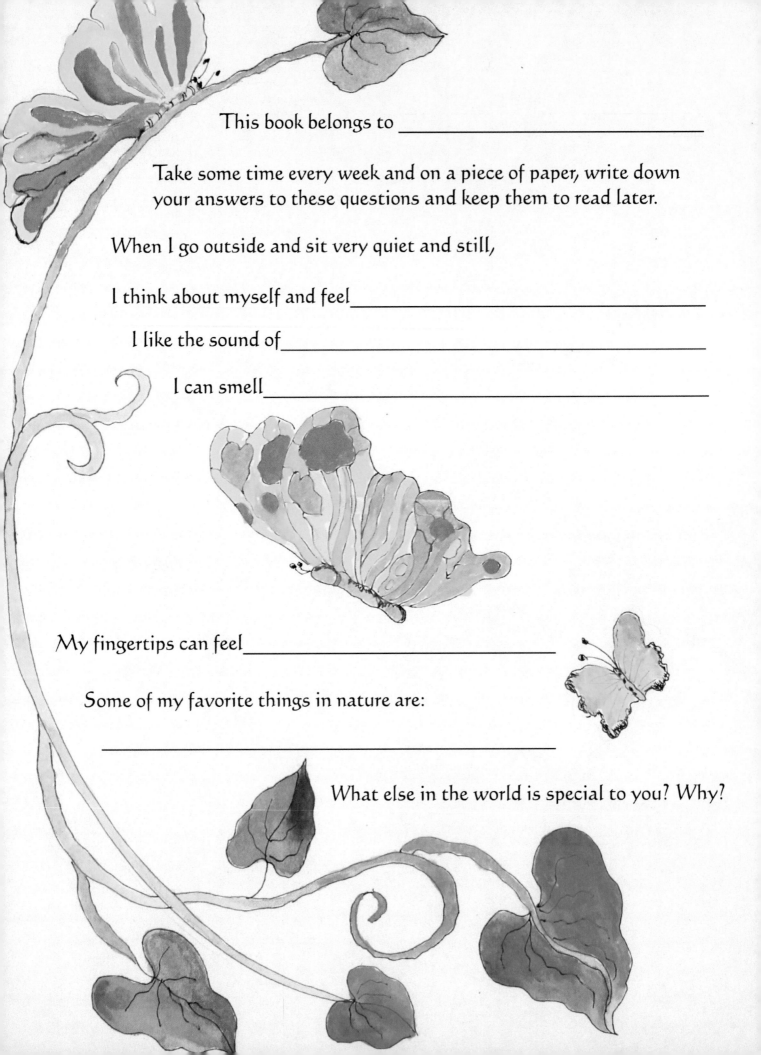

This book belongs to _____

Take some time every week and on a piece of paper, write down your answers to these questions and keep them to read later.

When I go outside and sit very quiet and still,

I think about myself and feel_____

I like the sound of_____

I can smell_____

My fingertips can feel_____

Some of my favorite things in nature are:

_____

What else in the world is special to you? Why?

Made in the USA
Coppell, TX
21 April 2022